SQUARE CAT ABC

Written and illustrated by

Elizabeth Schoonmaker

ALADDIN

NEW YORK   LONDON   TORONTO   SYDNEY   NEW DELHI

FOR MOM

ALADDIN • An imprint of Simon & Schuster Children's Publishing Division • 1230 Avenue of the Americas, New York, NY 10020 • First Aladdin hardcover edition December 2014 • Copyright © 2014 by Elizabeth Schoonmaker • All rights reserved, including the right of reproduction in whole or in part in any form. • ALADDIN is a trademark of Simon & Schuster, Inc., and related logo is a registered trademark of Simon & Schuster, Inc. • For information about special discounts for bulk purchases, please contact Simon & Schuster Special Sales at 1-866-506-1949 or business@simonandschuster.com. • The Simon & Schuster Speakers Bureau can bring authors to your live event. For more information or to book an event contact the Simon & Schuster Speakers Bureau at 1-866-248-3049 or visit our website at www.simonspeakers.com. • Designed by Karin Paprocki • The text of this book was set in Museo. • The illustrations for this book were rendered in Watercolor, gouache, watercolor pencils, ink. • Manufactured in China 0914 SCP • 2 4 6 8 10 9 7 5 3 1 • This book has been cataloged with the Library of Congress • ISBN 978-1-4424-9895-2 • ISBN 978-1-4424-9896-9 (eBook)

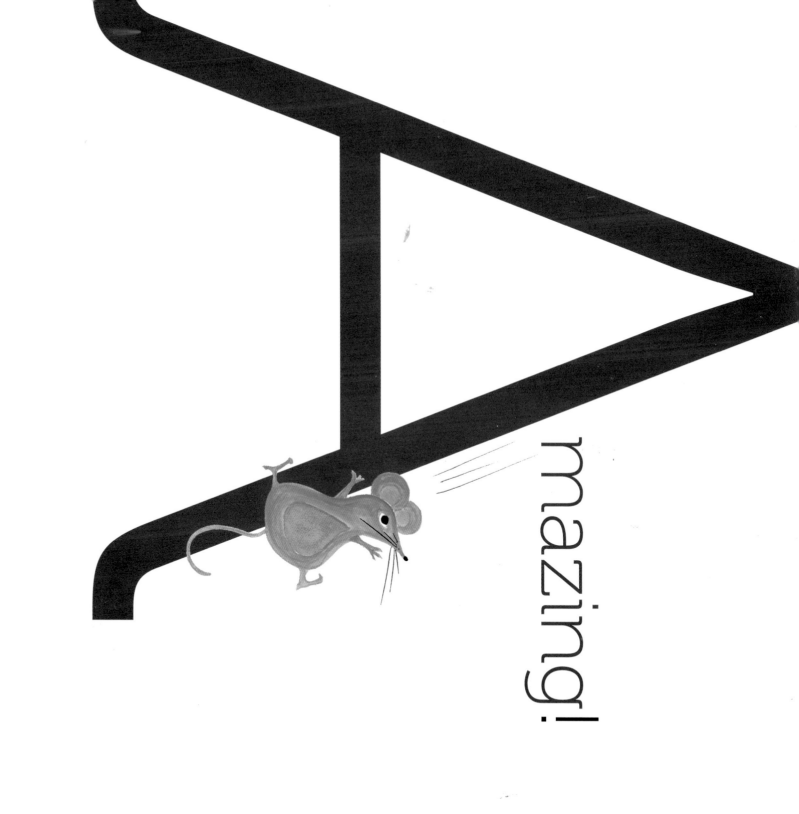

mazing!

A big square

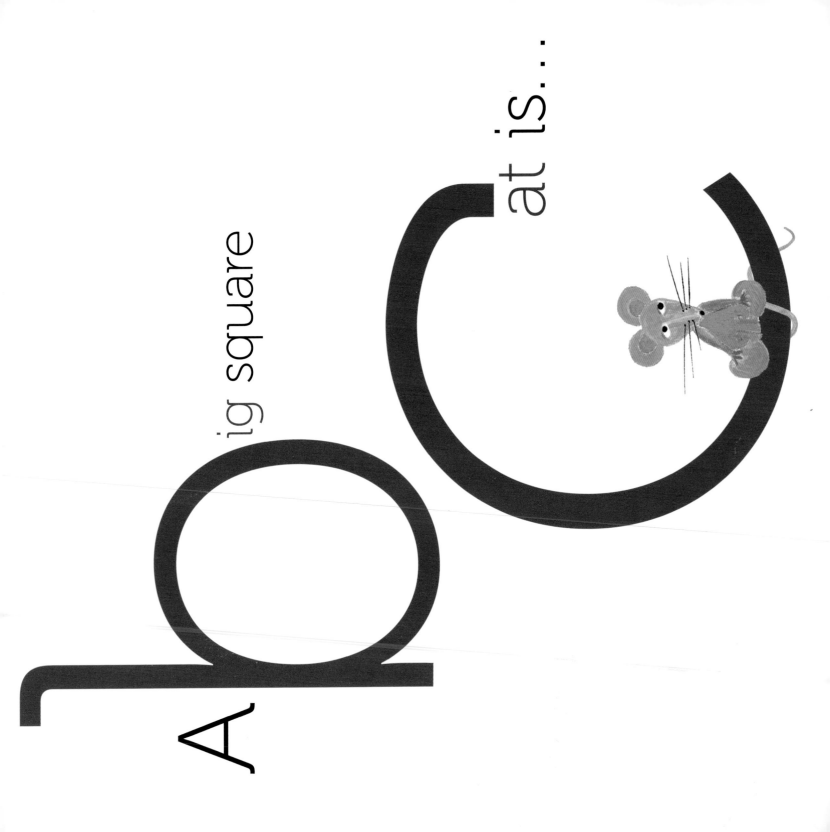

at is . . .

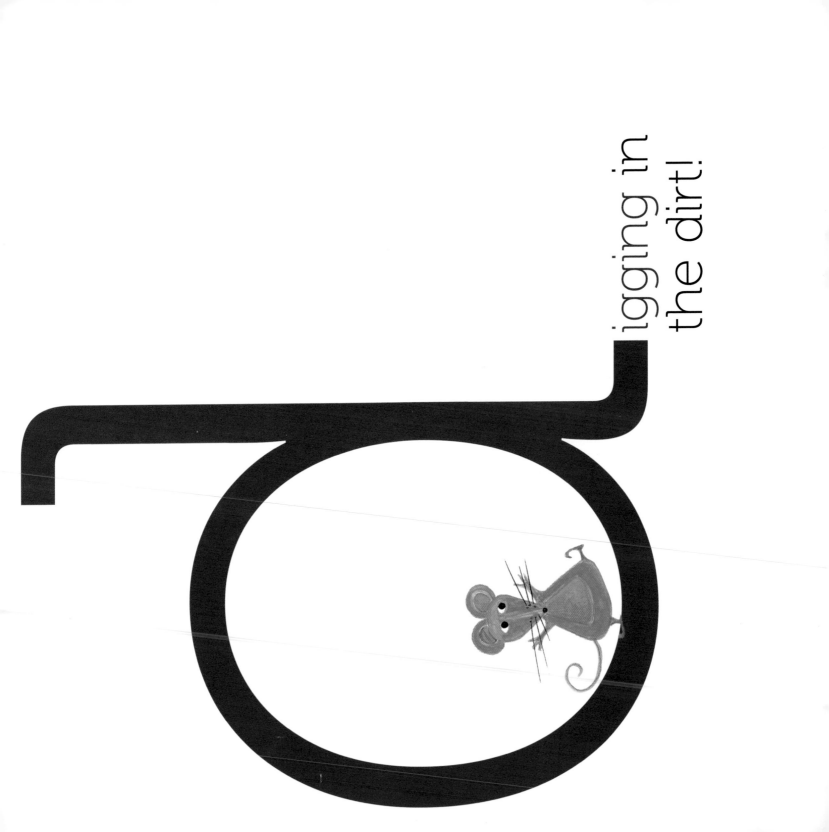

igging in
the dirt!

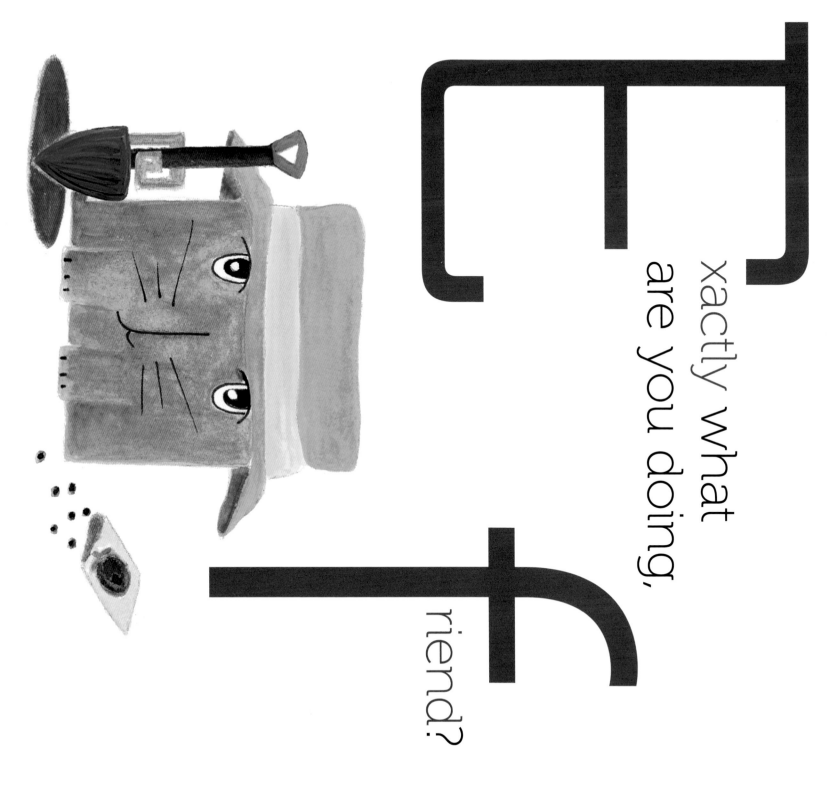

E xactly what
are you doing,

riend?

ardening.

ooray!

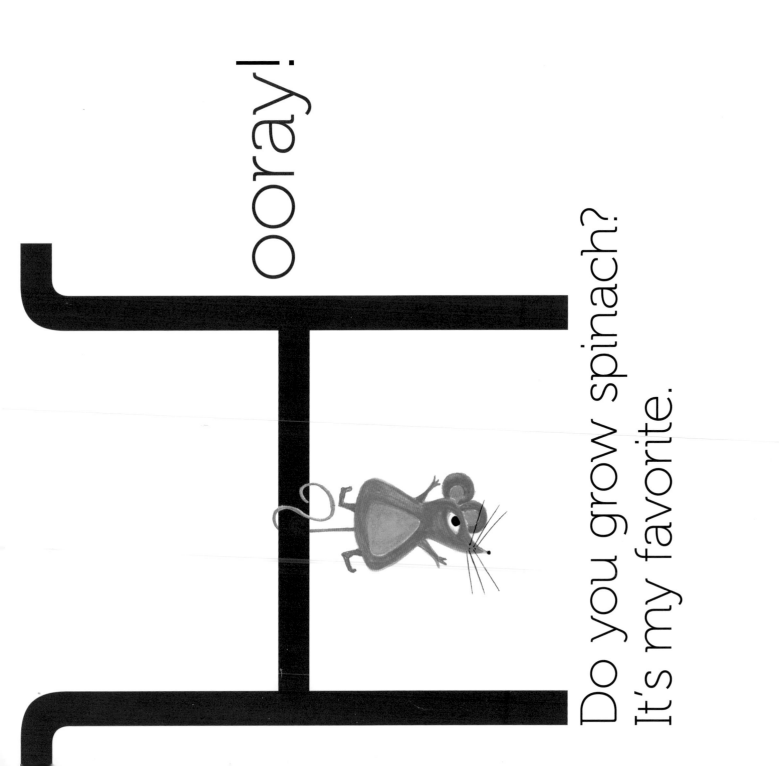

Do you grow spinach?
It's my favorite.

CK!

I grow all vegetables, but I DON'T like spinach.

ust green,
leafy
spinach
for me.

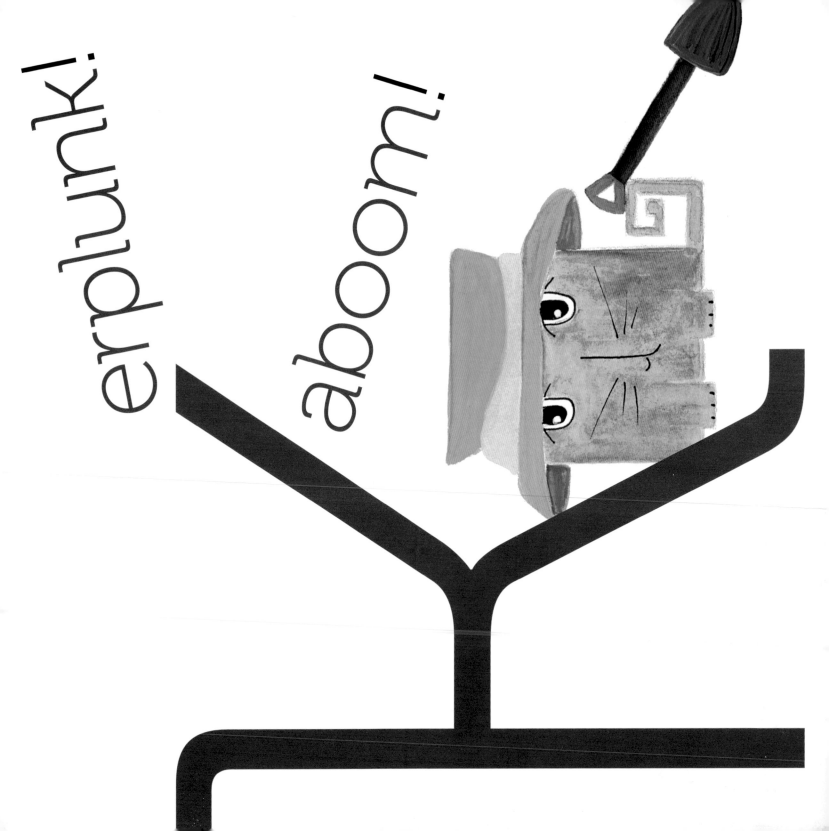

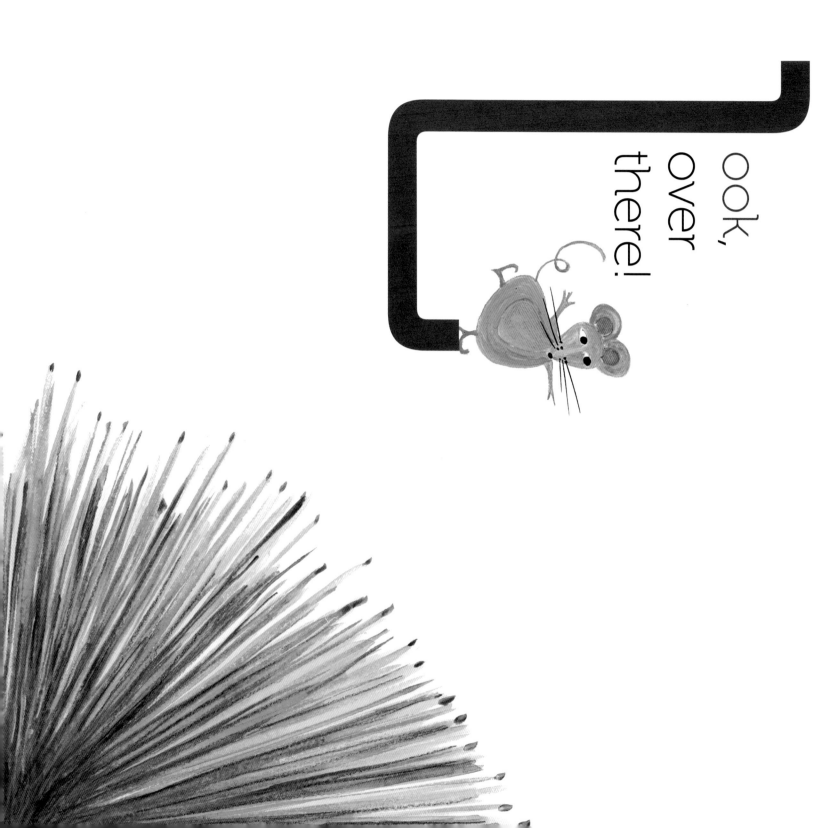

Look, over there!

Oh my! It's a ...

Oo! It can't be.

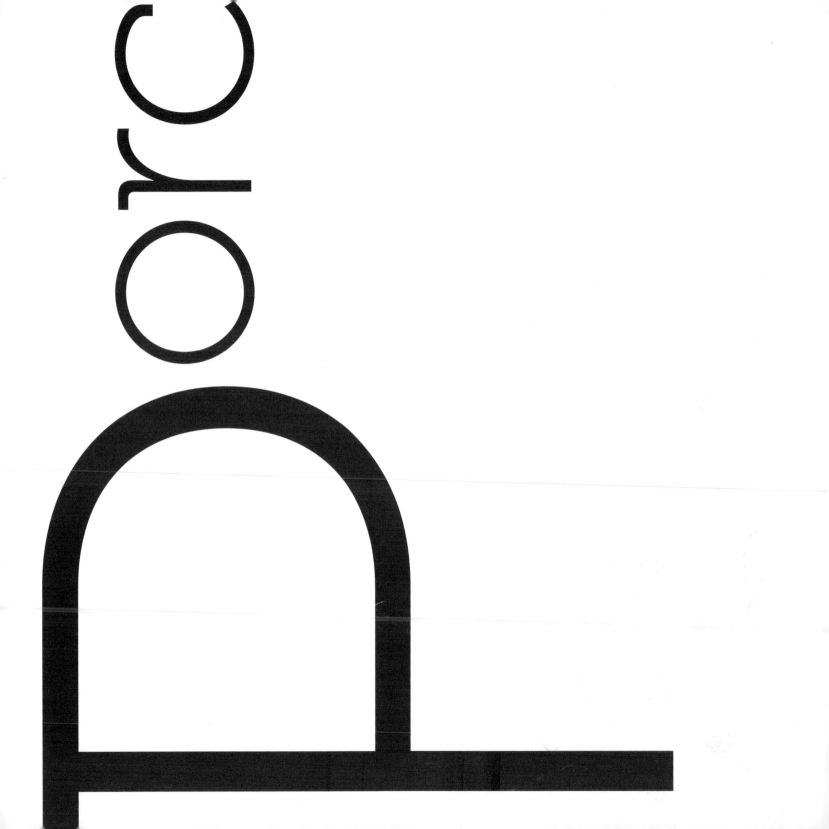

upine!

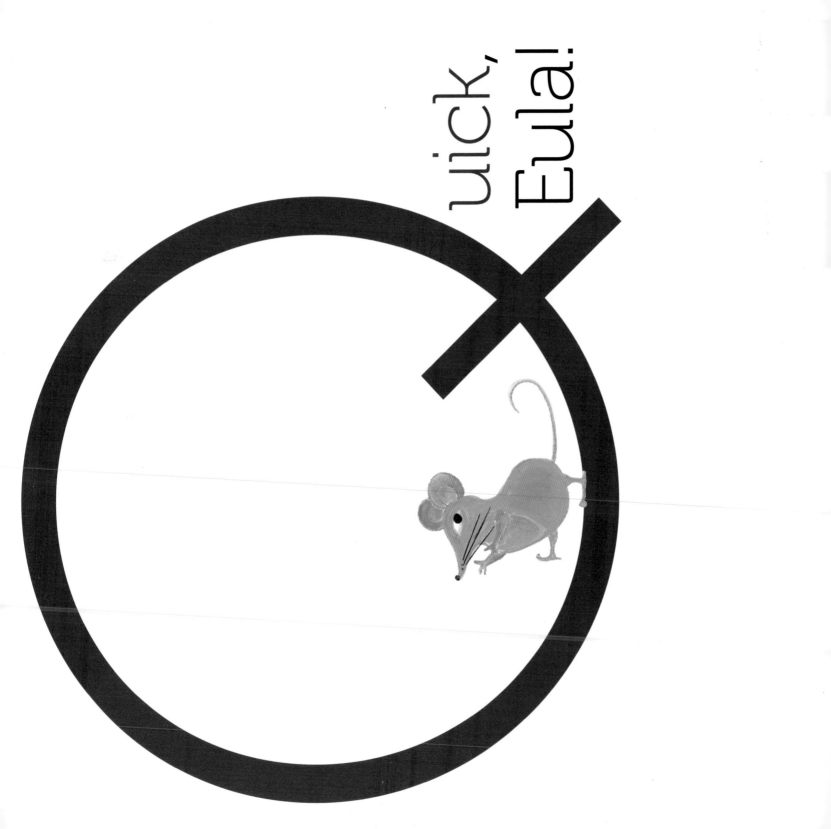

uick, Eula!

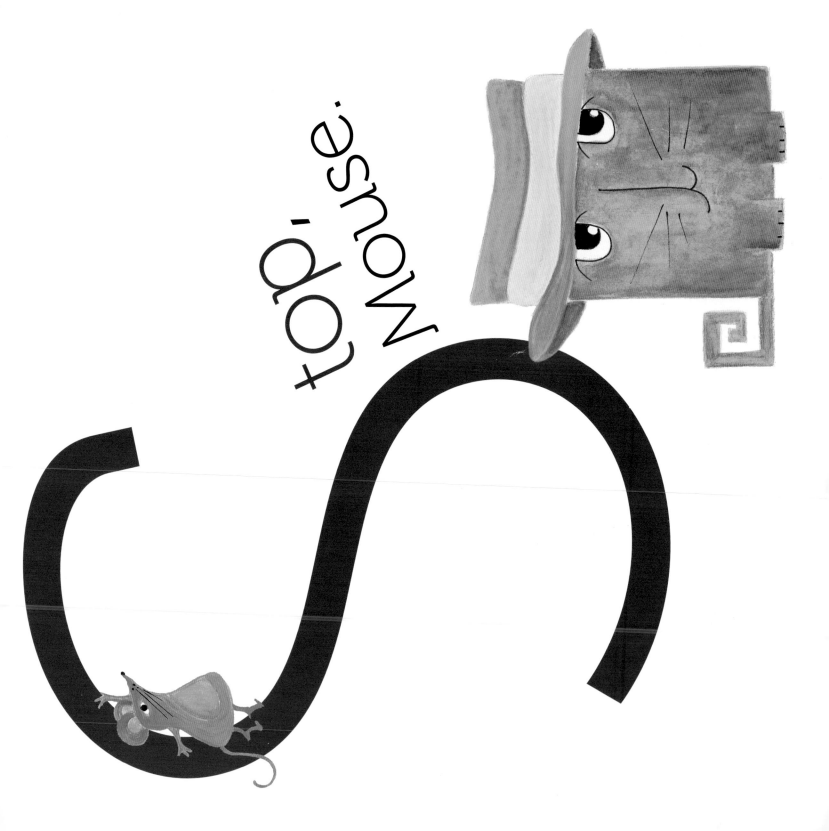

That porcupine is my friend.

ruly?
Look, your friend
is eating spinach, too.

nbelievable!
Why don't
you try a leaf,
Square Cat?

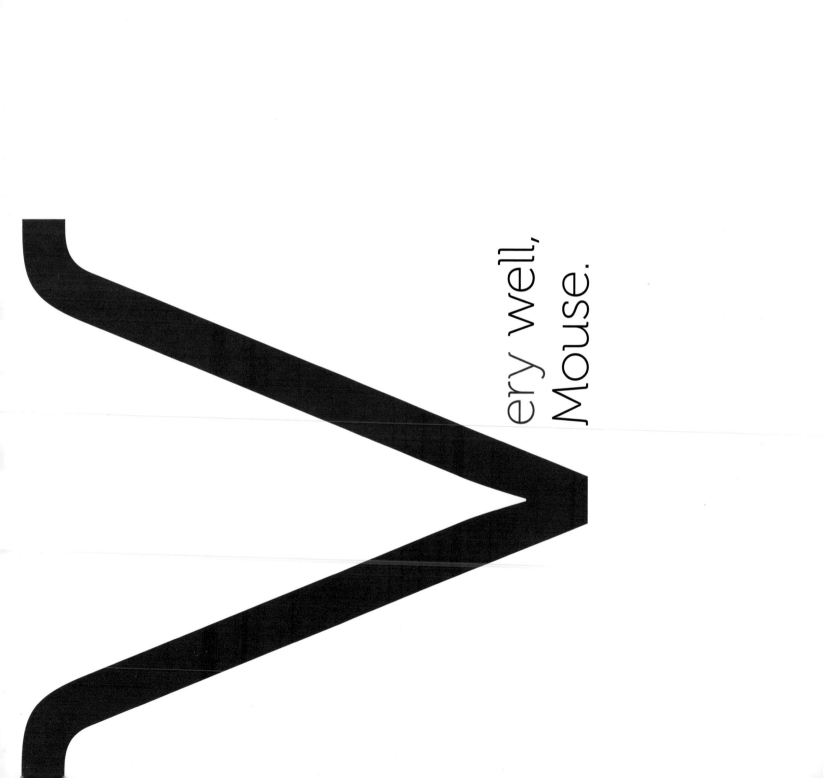

ery well, Mouse.

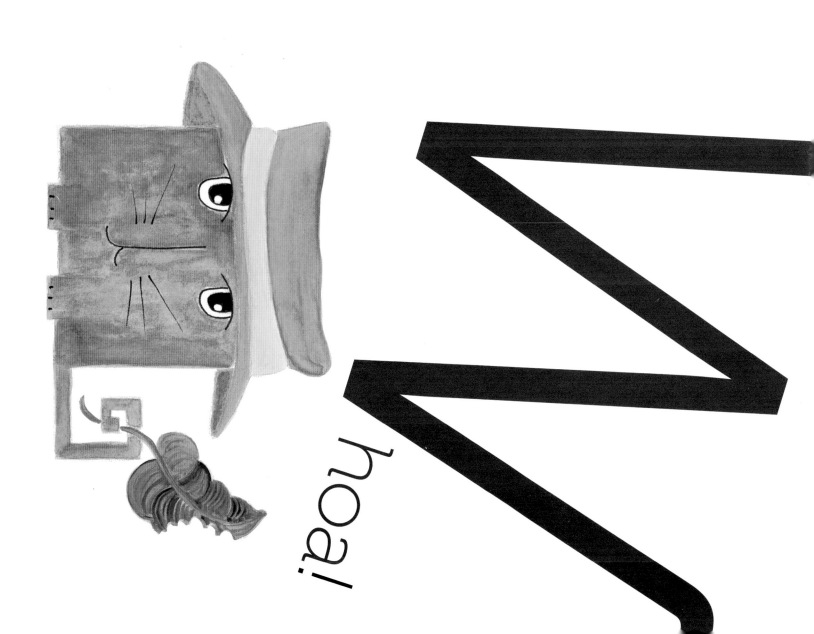

noel

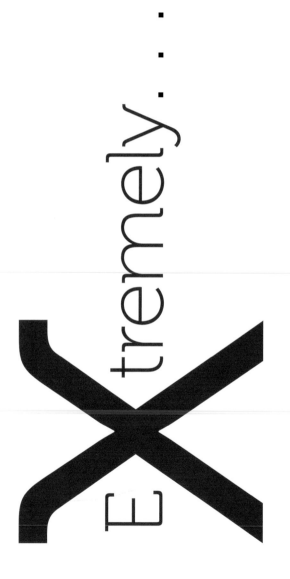

EXtremely. . . .

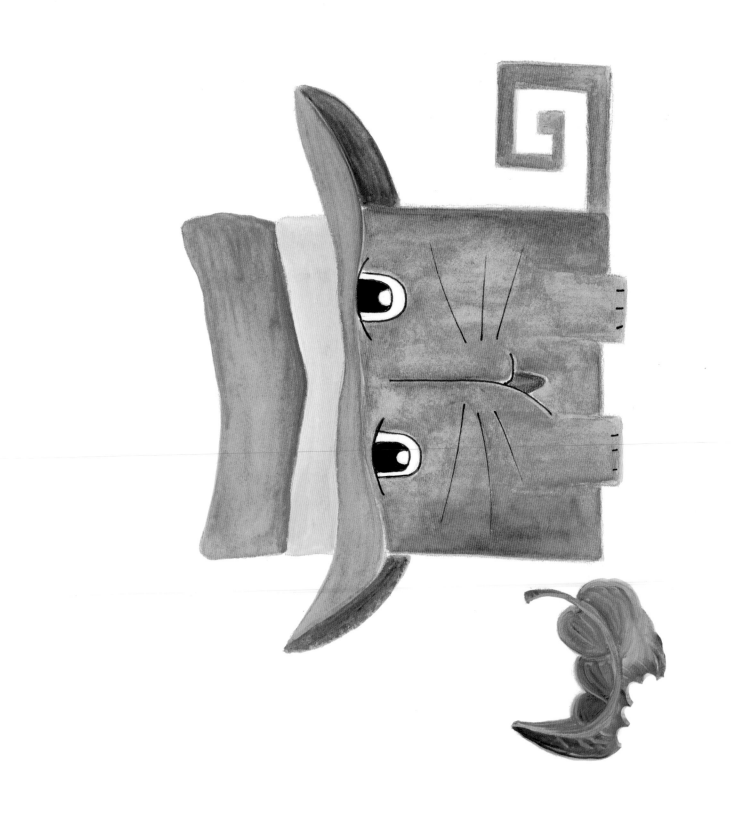

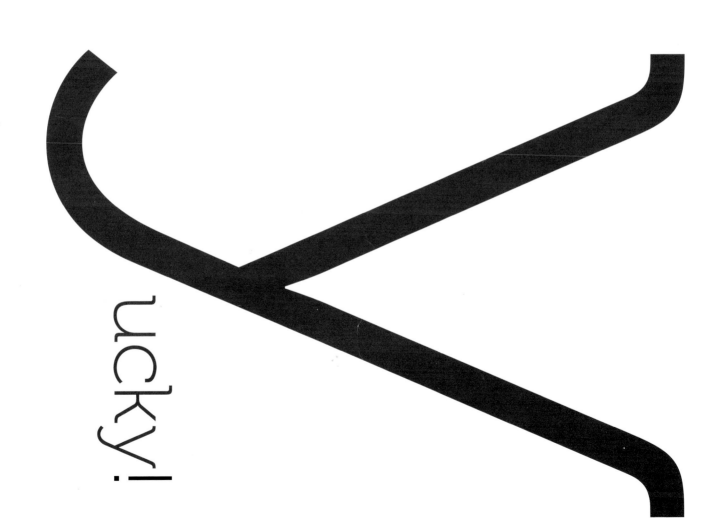

uckyl